THE PRINCE AND THE POLESTAR

Retold and
Illustrated by
Kosa Ely

CHANDRA

Published by Chandra
an imprint of Arts of Vaisnava Culture
P.O. Box 2272
Alachua, Florida 32616
phone and fax: 904-462-0137
www.chandramedia.com

Cover and interior design by Mayapriya Long, Bookwrights,
www.bookwrights.com

Library of Congress Cataloging-in-Publication Data

Ely, Kosa, 1960-
    The prince and the polestar / retold and illustrated by Kosa Ely
    p. cm.
Summary: Wishing to rule a great kingdom, young Prince Dhruva goes into the forest in search of Lord Narayana, encounters wild animals and saintly sages, performs severe austerities, and eventually gains a greater treasure than he ever imagined.
ISBN 0-9669268-1-1
(1.Folklore—India) L. Title.
PZ8.1.E55 Pr 2000
398.2'0954'02—dc21   00-091956 CIP

5 4 3 2 1
Printed in Hong Kong

For my children
Malini devi and Sri Gauramani
May Prince Dhruva be your hero.

$\mathcal{M}$other! Who's that coming to our forest!" asked the young tiger cub.

"It's a child, a human child," his mother answered, realizing her young cubs had never seen one before.

"Hmmm, I wonder why he's all alone. If you two can be quiet, we'll follow him and find out."

The mother tiger moved silently through the tall green grass while her cubs leaped playfully behind her. The boy strode fearlessly down the forest path, not noticing the animals and birds who followed.

The peacock announced to the others, "It appears as if our young visitor is looking for something or someone of utmost importance. He shows no concern for us, and no fear for himself. Although he is barefoot and without jewels, I am certain he is from a royal family."

After walking a great distance, the boy stopped and looked around. In a clear, strong voice he called out, "Lord Narayana, are You here? Please, Lord Narayana, please show Yourself to me." After a few minutes, he sat down.

The tiger cubs landed near the boy's feet as they tumbled about in their play. Seeing the mother tiger and other animals closely watching him, the boy turned to them and asked, "Have you seen Lord Narayana? Do you know where He is? Can any of you tell me where to find Him?"

"The sages I know meditate on Lord Narayana within their hearts," the deer answered. "That is how they find Him."

"I have heard," the wolf said thoughtfully, "the Lord appears to those who serve Him with faith and devotion."

The mother tiger spoke to discourage the boy. "I've never heard of a child risking his life for such a quest. Has your mother allowed you to come here alone, or did you leave home without permission?"

"I have my mother's permission to be here," the boy said defensively. "She wants me to find Lord Narayana. Now my father, the King—I don't care about his permission—not after what he did to me."

"The King!" exclaimed the parrots.

The peacock stepped forward. "Young Prince," he said, taking a bow, "it is an honor to meet you. Welcome to our forest. We will do all we can to help you." The others nodded in agreement. "Please, tell us more about yourself," the peacock insisted, "and about your search for Lord Narayana."

"You really want to know?" asked the prince.

"Yes, yes!" they answered all at once.

"My name is Prince Dhruva. My father, King Uttanapada, rules this earth. My mother is the noble Queen Suniti, and my great-grandfather is the powerful Lord Brahma, creator of this universe."

"Oh my!" said the parrot, more surprised than ever.

"But why are you here? What happened?" asked the tiger cubs impatiently.

"It all started the other day," Dhruva said, "when my brother Uttama and I were playing in the royal assembly hall. We ran toward the throne where our father was sitting with Uttama's mother, Queen Suruchi. Uttama got there first and Father lifted him onto his lap. He hugged Uttama and patted his cheeks. I wanted to get on Father's lap, too, but when I held out my arms, Father ignored me. When I started to climb up, Queen Suruchi stood up and shouted at me, 'Dhruva! Why are you trying to sit with Uttama? You are not worthy to sit there because you are not my son. I am the king's favorite queen. If you want to sit on your father's lap or on the throne you'll have to worship Lord Narayana. If He blesses you, then perhaps in your next life you can be born as my son.'

"I looked at my father. He looked away from me. He said nothing and did nothing. His silence hurt even more than the queen's harsh words.

"A powerful anger swelled up inside me. My whole body felt like it was on fire, and I could hardly breathe. I turned away, never wanting to see them again. I ran as fast as I could to find my mother."

"As soon as my mother saw me she lifted me onto her lap and held me close. I was crying so hard I couldn't speak. A few minutes later one of our servants came in and told her what Queen Suruchi said to me, and how my father remained silent.

"My mother started crying, too, saying, 'We should never wish for the unhappiness of others, even if they have hurt us. My dear son, the father of all fathers is Lord Narayana. If you really want to be happy, worship Him. Only He can fulfill your heart's desire. He will not fail you.'

"Then she told me how my great-grandfather, Lord Brahma, was able to create this whole universe by worshipping Lord Narayana. I started thinking that I should also worship the Lord to get what I want. That is why I've come here. And that is why I'm searching for Lord Narayana."

"I want to help you find Lord Narayana!" said the tiger cub.

"We'll all help you," said the peacock.

As evening came to the forest, the stars and moon began to appear in the darkening sky. The sweet smell of night–blooming jasmine filled the air. Prince Dhruva heard music, drifting down from the heavens, sweeter than any he had ever heard before. Listening intently, Dhruva searched the night sky for its source. Then, as if from no-where, the great sage Narada appeared.

Recognizing the sage, Prince Dhruva at once bowed down before him. Narada in turn blessed him, then asked, "Dhruva, other children your age are busy playing and having fun. Why have you become so troubled by Queen Suruchi's words? All of us receive both honor and dishonor in the course of our lives. It is better if you practice tolerance. Then you will feel satisfied. I know you have come to this forest in search of Lord Narayana, but that may take many lifetimes. For now, return home. When you are older I will help you."

"Sage Narada, please understand. Queen Suruchi's words were more than insults, they were sharp arrows that pierced my heart. I will not go home until I see Lord Narayana.

"I want to ask Him for a kingdom much greater than my father's. I want a position even greater than Lord Brahma's. You are the best devotee of Lord Narayana, surely you will help me."

Smiling at the young prince before him, Narada considered deeply, "This child wants a kingdom greater than any in the universe! He is so determined for this, he cannot understand what will really make him happy."

Narada then said to Dhruva, "Yes, only the Supreme Lord can fulfill such a great desire. Listen closely and I will tell you how to find Him."

Following Narada's instructions, Prince Dhruva set out for the Madhuvana forest. Along the way he told the animals, "I'm going to the bank of the Yamuna River in the forest of Madhuvana. In this holy place I am to bathe every day, sit quietly, and practice bhakti-yoga. The sage described the beautiful form of Lord Narayana within my heart. Now I know how to meditate on Him. And he taught me a sacred mantra to chant to gain the Lord's blessings."

"Will you teach it to us?" asked the peacock.

"Please, Dhruva, please!" begged the others.

"All right, repeat after me: Om…namo…bhagavate…vasudevaya." One by one, all of the animals and birds repeated the mantra as they followed Dhruva down the forest path.

"And then Lord Narayana will come?" asked the little monkey.

"Sage Narada said, 'When the Lord is pleased with your love for Him, then He will come.'"

The young prince followed Sage Narada's instructions very seriously. Fixing his mind on the beautiful form of the Lord within his heart, Dhruva soon conquered his mind and senses. No longer needing to eat or drink, he remained still, absorbed in thoughts of the Supreme Lord.

The tiger cubs complained to their mother, "Prince Dhruva doesn't play

with us anymore. He doesn't even notice us! How long will he just sit there?"

Perched on a nearby tree, the parrot said to her mate, "This child is the greatest yogi I have ever seen. It's been months since he ate any berries or fruits, and I can't remember when he last drank water. He's so still, I wonder if he's even breathing."

Indeed, by the end of the fifth month, Dhruva, who had captured the Supreme Lord within his heart, no longer needed to breathe. When Dhruva stopped breathing, the whole universe started trembling. From the highest planet down to the lowest, everyone began choking and gasping for air. The denizens of heaven, confused and frightened, went to Lord Narayana for help.

"My dear demigods," said the Lord, smiling, "because My devotee Dhruva is performing great penance to meet Me, the universal breathing has become choked. I will go at once to see him."

Dhruva had no idea he was upsetting everyone in the universe. He was completely absorbed in meditation on the Lord's beautiful form. Relishing this vision within his heart, he was unaware of anything else.

Then, suddenly, the Lord within disappeared.

In great distress, Dhruva opened his eyes.

There before him stood the Supreme Lord Narayana—illuminating all directions with His shimmering effulgence.

Overwhelmed by seeing his Lord face to face, Dhruva drank in the the Lord's beauty with his eyes. He fell flat upon the ground to offer respect as he embraced the Lord within his heart.

Although Dhruva wanted to offer wonderful prayers, he did not know how to begin. Lord Narayana, understanding his mind and heart, touched Dhruva's forehead with His transcendental conchshell. By that touch, Dhruva's worldly desires vanished and his heart over-flowed with love. Now purified, Dhruva began glorifying the Lord with excellent prayers. These prayers, filled with truth and wisdom, are still chanted today, though many ages of the earth have passed.

Dhruva looked up at Lord Narayana, whose glistening jewels sparkled like the stars in the sky. He said, "My Lord, only You can free me from birth and death. Please accept me as Your eternal servant. I have foolishly worshipped You for a kingdom and for power. Now that I see You before me there is nothing in this world that I want. You alone are the greatest treasure!"

"My dear Dhruva," the Lord said with affection, "I am very pleased with you, and I will grant all your desires. Behold the glowing Polestar shining brightly in the northern sky. This star, unlike any other, is My very own spiritual planet that will never be destroyed. From now on, it will be known as Dhruvaloka, and it will be your planet and kingdom to rule.

"When you are grown, your father will give you his kingdom here on earth. You will rule for many, many years without ever becoming old. At the end of your life, when it is time to leave this body, you will come to the Polestar, Dhruvaloka, to live with Me eternally. Your mother will also come and share your good fortune."

After being worshipped by Dhruva, the Lord mounted His bird carrier, Garuda, and soared upward beyond the heavens. Dhruva watched in awe until they could no longer be seen.

Although he had achieved everything he had wanted and more, Dhruva was stricken with grief.

Excited to congratulate the Prince, the animals and birds came running and flying over to him. Instead of celebrating, Prince Dhruva turned away and walked toward the river. "Wait here," the parrot said to the others, "I'll see if I can find out what's wrong."

Dhruva sat down on the bank of the river and began to weep. "How could I have been so foolish? I worshipped the Lord for something that will not last, and now I have a kingdom and a position I no longer want.

"Lord Narayana is so beautiful, kind and loving. All the wealth and power of this universe cannot compare with having Him! He is the greatest treasure. And now I have lost Him."

Dhruva cried for some time.

Hoping to see Lord Narayana again, Prince Dhruva looked up toward the heavens. The Lord's words came back to him, "Behold the glowing Polestar shining brightly in the northern sky. It is My very own spiritual planet that will never be destroyed. It will be your planet and kingdom to rule. At the end of your life you will come to Dhruvaloka and live with Me eternally."

Knowing he would again be with his Lord, he felt comforted.

"What will you do now?" asked the deer, whose voice and gentle manner reminded Dhruva of his mother.

"It's time for me to go home."

The tiger cubs shuffled their paws slowly, hoping to make their final journey with the prince last as long as possible. At the peacock's request they softly sang together, "Om namo bhagavate vasudevaya."

When the King learned from a messenger that Dhruva was returning from the forest, he could not believe his good fortune. For six long months the King had suffered, blaming himself for the absence of his son.

King Uttanapada gathered his family members, ministers and friends. They set out at once in a grand parade to meet Prince Dhruva and welcome him home.

As the royal procession neared, Dhruva turned to the animals and birds to say good-bye. "Thank you for everything. I will miss all of you." The tiger cubs jumped up on Dhruva, knocking him over. They all laughed, though tears of sadness filled their eyes.

"Don't forget!" Dhruva said, "When you see the Polestar in the night sky, remember Lord Narayana . . . remember everything we learned together."